FERGUS'S

BIG SPLASH

To my grandchildren:
Natalie, Zara, Chloe, Holly, Olivia and Jamie

Text and illustration copyright © Tony Maddox, 1996

Printed and bound in Belgium by Proost, for the publishers Piccadilly Press Ltd., U.K. 5 Castle Road, London NW1 8PR

A catalogue record for this book is available from the British Library

ISBN: 1 85340 382 2 (hardback)
1 85340 388 1 (paperback)

Tony Maddox lives in Worcestershire. Piccadilly Press publish his tremendously successful books, *Spike the Sparrow Who Couldn't Sing*, *Fergus the Farmyard Dog* and *Fergus's Upside-down Day*.

FERGUS THE FARMYARD DOG
ISBN: 1 85340 174 9

FERGUS'S UPSIDE-DOWN DAY
ISBN: 1 85340 284 2

SPIKE THE SPARROW WHO COULDN'T SING
ISBN: 1 85340 196 X

FERGUS'S
BIG SPLASH

Tony Maddox

Piccadilly Press • London

Fergus was looking for Farmer Bob.
He wasn't in the hayfield.

He wasn't in the big barn.

Fergus asked the animals.
"Moo!" said the cow.
"Oink, Oink!" suggested the pigs.
"Cluck, Cluck, Cluck!" added the hen.
"Quack, Quack!" agreed the ducks.

"Humph!" thought Fergus.
"He must have gone fishing!"
So he went to look.
And the cow, the three pigs,
the two ducks and the hen
followed him...

...through the tall grass of the meadow...

...over the stile and into the dark wood...

...until they came to the big pond.
Fergus climbed into an old boat
moored by the bank, to get
a better view.
The cow climbed in after him, followed
by the three pigs, the two ducks and
the hen.

The boat drifted to the middle of the pond. The animals Mooed and Oinked and Quacked and Clucked and the boat rocked. Everyone was having a great time... except Fergus!

"I do wish they would keep still!"
he worried.

But they didn't...
and the boat rocked more...and more
and more...until SPLASH!

It tipped up completely, tumbling everyone into the water.

Farmer Bob woke with a start.
He'd fallen asleep in the shade
of a big tree. "What's that?" he said.
He turned to see...

the cow paddling in the water,
the pigs rolling in the mud,
the ducks playing in the reeds,
the hen pecking in the grass...
and a very wet Fergus!

"Fergus," said Farmer Bob.
"What have you been up to?"
The other animals gathered round.
It looked like Fergus was in trouble.

"Well," thought Fergus.
"At least I did find Farmer Bob!"
And he shook himself dry and trotted
back to the farm.

That was the second soaking
the animals had that day!